Jake
and His Cousin
Sidney

Jake's Dad

This Jake book
belongs to

....

For Norman,
my friend – and my accountant –
with love

This edition first published 2002 by
Walker Books Ltd, 87 Vauxhall Walk
London SE11 5HJ

10 9 8 7 6 5 4 3 2 1

© 1994, 2002 Simon James

The right of Simon James to be
identified as author of this work has
been asserted by him in accordance
with the Copyright, Designs and
Patents Act 1988

This book has been typeset
in Usherwood ITC

Printed in Hong Kong

British Library Cataloguing in Publication Data: a catalogue record
for this book is available from the British Library

ISBN 0-7445-8998-3

With warm thanks to Sian for photography

Jake
and His Cousin Sidney

Simon James

WALKER BOOKS
AND SUBSIDIARIES
LONDON • BOSTON • SYDNEY

Jake was difficult.
Jake was a problem.
And Jake didn't like babies. All they
seemed to do was cry and smell something
awful. So you can imagine how Jake felt
one day when he had to take care
of his cousin Sidney.

Jake did his best.
He fed Sidney his baby food.
He even changed Sidney's nappy.
Then Jake's mother said
it was time for Sidney's bath.

Jake carried Sidney upstairs to the bathroom
and turned on the taps.
The bath always took such a long time to fill.
So Jake thought he'd go to his room
and read for a while.
Sidney waited.

And he waited.
In fact, it was quite some time
before Jake remembered Sidney's bath.
Jake ran out of his bedroom towards the
bathroom door ...

only to find Sidney floating out on the
crest of a gigantic wave.
"Be brave, Sidney!" called Jake, as he jumped
on board …

and rode the rapids downstairs to the hall.

Meanwhile, in the living room, Jake's father
began to wonder what the loud slurping noise
was in the hallway.
He got up from his chair and walked
towards the door.

Jake and Sidney, meanwhile, were beginning to wonder just how much MORE water would fill the hall.

Fortunately, Jake's father opened the living room door just in time.
"Hooray!" said Jake.

At that moment, Jake's sister came home from her Brownies meeting. She'd just reached the front door when suddenly …

out burst her mother, her father, several pieces of furniture and, at the top of a huge tidal wave, Jake and his cousin Sidney. Jake's sister was drenched.

Jake's parents stood helplessly
as their beautiful home,
now filled to the brim with water,
slowly lifted up from the ground and
started to float down the road.

That night Jake's father had to check the whole family into the local hotel. He made sure that Jake and Sidney shared a room by themselves.

But Jake didn't mind taking care of his brave little cousin.
And Sidney certainly didn't cry.
He knew ...

he'd grow up to be just like Jake.

love from
Jake and Sidney

SIMON JAMES is an award-winning author and illustrator of books for children and a regular speaker in schools and at festivals across the UK and the USA. His books for Walker include *Sally and the Limpet*; *My Friend Whale*; *The Wild Woods*; *Dear Greenpeace*; *The Birdwatchers*; *Days Like This*, which was shortlisted for the Kate Greenaway Medal; *Leon and Bob*, for which he won the Smarties Book Prize Silver Medal and The New York Times Best Illustrated Book of the Year; and two more stories about Jake: *The Day Jake Vacuumed* and *Jake and the Babysitter*. Simon lives in south Devon.

Other stories about naughty Jake:

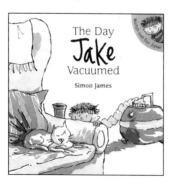

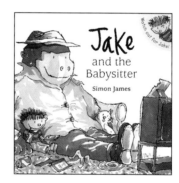

ISBN 0-7445-9400-6 (pb)   ISBN 0-7445-8999-1 (pb)